THE ADVENTURES OF ARAB

THE ADVENTURES OF ARAB

LOUIS SLOBODKIN

THE MACMILLAN COMPANY
NEW YORK   1946

TO FLORENCE

MICHAEL AND LARRY'S

MOTHER

CONTENTS

1. Two Tales in Horse Arabic

IN A FAR CORNER OF THE PARK there was once a fine old merry-go-round. It was an all-horse merry-go-round. That is to say, there were no swan boats, flowered sleds, or anything like that to ride on. Only horses! Beautiful prancing horses who not only went round and round with the music that came from the center of the merry-go-round! All these horses pranced round and round, up and down, round and round, and up and down.

Now you can easily understand why all the children who came to the park every sunny day always had to ride on the

7

merry-go-round at least once, and some twice—and I've heard of boys who had even three rides on the horses on the same day!

Mr. Timothy was the old man who sold and collected tickets and took care of all the horses on the merry-go-round. The children never called the merry-go-round a merry-go-round. They would say as they walked through the park, "We're going to ride on Mr. Timothy's horses." And that's what they called the merry-go-round—Mr. Timothy's horses.

Now Mr. Timothy's horses were so popular with all the children, and so many boys and girls wanted to ride at the same time on their favorite horses that, even though there were twelve horses on that merry-go-round and they kept going round and round and up and down all day long, there was always a long line of children waiting for their turn to ride. Some had to go home in tears on some fine sunny days because they'd overslept and were too far down the line to get even one ride on Mr. Timothy's wonderful horses.

Mr. Timothy was a kindly man and he hated to see the children going home disappointed. One early spring day while the children were still going to school and it was too cold to come to the park, Mr. Timothy moved the twelve horses a little closer together on the merry-go-round and brought in a beautiful spirited horse and set him up in the empty space.

And since my story is about that horse and not so much about all the others I'll tell you his name. It was Arab. That was the name that was painted in fine scrolly gold letters on his bridle and his bright red saddle.

Arab became the favorite with all the children. And, though they still waited in line to ride on the merry-go-round, they would not go home feeling too bad if they hadn't had a chance to ride, because it was a joy just to look at Arab. He'd prance so gaily as he swung round and round! Arab seemed to go swifter, as he went round and round, than all the other horses, and he easily jumped twice as high as he went up and down.

But Arab was not happy, and the only one who knew his

secret was an old coach horse whose master, Mr. Bill, usually stopped and talked to Mr. Timothy in the early morning when children were just drinking their orange juice.

The old coach horse naturally had old horse sense. He knew there was something different about Arab and, as he stood nibbling the grass along the path one morning, he heard a deep sigh like the sound the wind makes going through the treetops. The old horse lifted his head and looked toward the merry-go-round. Again he heard the sighing voice:

"Heavy is the burden, sad my lot.
Mayhap it's Fate . . ."

"And maybe it's not," said the old coach horse, completing the rhyme.

Arab, for it was he who had begun the old Arabian poem, said in a low voice, "Salaam, Old One. How is it that you know Horse Arabic, the language of my homeland, and the poetry of its sages?"

In case you don't know, "Salaam" means "Peace." That's the way everyone greeted everyone else in Arab's homeland, whether he meant it or not. And everyone responded, "Peace be with you," as the coach horse did.

"Salaam alaykoum," said the old horse. "Young One, you are not alone. I too have come from the land of the great deserts, the date palms, and the most wonderful horses in the world. Oh yes, I too am an Arabian."

The old horse sighed and a large tear splashed down on the green grass he was nibbling.

"You'd not know it," continued the old coach horse after he'd pulled himself together a bit and blinked the tears from his eyes. "You would not know that once I too was young and spirited and dashed across the sun-drenched desert carrying bejeweled princes on my strong curved back. Now would you? From the look of me now, I mean."

Arab looked at the bony old horse peering sadly through the iron fence that separated the merry-go-round from the road, and politely said, "Why, yes . . . I might."

That kind remark cheered the old horse up and he told Arab his story—how once he had been a beautiful young horse in Arabia and how he'd finally become what he was. It was a long, rambling, sad story that anyone could believe because the old horse told it so sincerely with very little exaggeration.

"Now tell me your story," said the old coach horse, feeling a lot better now that he'd unburdened himself. "Just the highlights—the important parts. I can well imagine the rest."

"I don't know where to begin," said Arab.

"Begin at the beginning, naturally," insisted the old horse. "For example, since it's completely unnatural for a wooden horse (you are carved of wood, if you'll excuse my saying so)—well, it's a little strange for a wooden horse to speak and to understand the speech of others. Now you could begin by telling me when you received the gift of speech and understanding. That's a good place to begin."

"I haven't thought that was so strange," said Arab. "You see, I was carved from a root of one of the wonder trees that border the mirage pool in the center of the great desert. Those trees are different, you know—since they can move it's only natural anyone carved from their wood can talk, particularly one who is carved from the roots."

"Yes," said the coach horse slowly.

"You sound doubtful," said Arab. "I'm a little doubtful about that part of my story too. Let me begin again. Many years ago a very old wizard was lost in the great desert. As he lay dying of thirst he saw the mirage of the pool surrounded by wonder trees. With his last ounce of strength, which he had kept hidden away in the heel of his right sandal for such an emergency, he arose and ran to drink his fill in the crystal-

clear strawberry-flavored waters of the pool. That saved his life, for he was very thirsty. After he had refreshed himself, he was terribly hungry and wondered where his next meal was coming from. Since it so happens he was seated under my mother's tree, and wonder trees give people what they wonder about—like wishing wells give wishes . . . or . . ."

"Or hopping fields give hops," suggested the coach horse.

"Yes—or hopping fields give hops—my mother's wonder tree quickly blossomed and perfumed the air with the nicest next meal anyone could want. After the old wizard had eaten he decided that, although he was quite a bit out of practice, he'd try again to do one of those magical things wizards always do to get themselves out of trouble. Since he'd lost most of the things out of his bag of tricks as he wandered in the desert, and now had only a few vials of magic oil and a sharp little knife which had got caught in the lining of his bag, he decided to carve a beautiful swift steed from one of the exposed roots of my mother's tree. I believe he planned to ride back to his home in Bagdad."

"And you are that beautiful swift steed?" asked the coach horse.

"Yes," said Arab modestly, "I am. But the old wizard worked very slowly, since his knife was so small and wonder wood is so hard. By the time he finished and rubbed me down with a few drops of his magic oil he was completely exhausted. And he rubbed so weakly it was years before the oil sunk in and had any effect. Meanwhile the wizard became impatient waiting for me to come to life as he sat there alone under the wonder trees, and he traded me to the owner of a caravan that was traveling across the desert—for a camel ride to Bagdad.

"In time I was sold to a merchant who traded me to a sea captain for a bale of hay (not good fresh hay either), and I passed through many hands and traveled to many places until good Mr. Timothy bought me for this merry-go-round."

"You've had an adventurous life for one so young," said the old coach horse. "How does it happen you are unhappy now?"

"Well, yes, I have had an adventurous life, but I'm not

15

really young. I just don't show my years," said Arab. "Oh, I'm happier here than I've ever been. The children are all gay and wonderful riders, and Mr. Timothy is very kind. But I'm one who likes to be on the move. I like to see new things. Why, do you know, although I lived in this park almost all summer, this little clump of trees and that stretch of road is all I've seen of this big city we live in?"

The old coach horse champed his teeth and shook his head in sympathy.

"Yes, all I do is go round and round and up and down all day long," said Arab mournfully. "And, though I go as swift as I can and as high as I might without going through the roof of this old merry-go-round, I stay in the same place. It's getting monotonous."

"Patience, Young One, patience," said the coach horse.

"Patience is the virtue of the aged," murmured Arab. Then he noticed the old coach horse's reproachful look, and he added, "No offense meant. I don't want to appear ungrateful to Mr. Timothy or any of the children. But if I were to have only one day to travel around the city to see this Bagdad of the West—I believe I would be happy."

For a few minutes there was a silence between them. Then the old coach horse spoke again.

"Young One, perhaps something can be arranged. Perhaps you will get that day of freedom—yes, perhaps you will."

"How?" asked Arab eagerly.

"Well," said the coach horse as he slowly chewed a wisp

16

of grass, "what would you think of becoming a coach horse for a day—of taking my place between these shafts sometime? Of course we coach horses do not see the whole city. That is, we're not allowed on subways and not permitted to go into the big library. We travel only along the more fashionable avenues. But we do see the rich shop windows, the fine buildings, the bright lights, and the better restaurants—in all, the cream of the city so to speak."

"Oh, that would be wonderful!" said the delighted Arab. "When could I start? Tell me quickly. Oh, how kind you are!"

The coach horse swallowed the grass, and a slow smile lit up his tired old face.

"Patience, Young One, patience. And stop bounding up and down so. My master and Mr. Timothy are looking this way. There, now you've done it. Your jumping around makes Mr. Timothy think something's gone wrong with the machinery that makes the merry-go-round go round, and he's coming to fix it. My master, Mr. Bill, has tapped out his pipe on his shoe; he's climbing up on his coach seat. Well, here we go—we're off. We'll talk about this again soon. Good-by."

"Good-by," said Arab.

And the old coach horse clopped down the road, turning his head every now and then to smile back and wink at happy Arab. Mr. Timothy put away the monkey wrench he'd picked out of his toolbox; for Arab had restrained his joyous bounding about, and the merry-go-round had stopped shaking.

2. The Coach Horse's Secret Plans

FROM THEN ON, every morning through that long summer, Arab looked forward to the daily visits of the old coach horse.

Every morning he breathlessly whispered, "Is this the day, Old One? Is this the day of my freedom?"

"No, not yet," the old coach horse answered. "There are many things to be arranged. I'm working on it."

"What's being done? Please tell me," said the impatient Arab. "Perhaps there's something I can do to help."

"Well, it's not so much doing things as thinking things," said the old coach horse. "Thinking and planning, that is."

18

"Ah me," said Arab sadly.

"Cheer up, Young One. I'll tell you the plans as far as I've gone. Remember they're secret plans, and you mustn't tell them to anyone. Mr. Timothy, Mr. Bill, the children, and the merry-go-round horses would all feel bad if they learned about this."

"Why?"

"Well, naturally they'd all feel bad if they knew you were unhappy here and wanted to be free."

Arab pondered that thought a moment. Then he said, "I don't believe they'd all feel like that . . . particularly the horses."

"Why not the horses?" asked the coach horse.

"Because, as you must have seen by this time," said Arab, "they lack the gift of speech and understanding."

"I can't see as well as I once did," said the coach horse. "But you must admit that all the others—Mr. Timothy and the children especially—would feel uncomfortable if they knew you felt you were chained to their service. I'm sure their consciences would bother them as they rode round and round on your shiny back."

"But I'm not chained," said Arab.

"What was that?"

"I said I am not chained," repeated Arab. "See, it's just this metal band around my middle that holds me to this old merry-go-round."

"Oh my," said the coach horse, with a hopeless look on his long face. "Oh, that's bad! That's something I hadn't figured on. I'm afraid all our plans are ruined. We might as well forget the whole thing."

"Why?" Arab almost shouted in his distress.

"Shush," hissed the coach horse as he quickly looked toward his master and Mr. Timothy gently swinging on the iron gate while they talked the morning away. "Quietly, please, Young One. As you know, I'm nearsighted; but I always believed all you merry-go-round horses were tied to your posts—as anyone else is. Either tied or chained. I've learned a long time ago how to slip my halter, or get back into it if I wanted to. Any old horse knows how. But that iron band around your middle—I can't tell you how to break through that. Now if it were a rope or chain it would be simple. Take a chain now—you start nibbling at one of the weaker links."

"But I can get out of this metal band," said Arab.

"You can?"

"Why, yes, easily," said Arab, with a touch of pride in his voice. "Before Mr. Timothy set me up on these posts he measured me carefully around my chest to be sure this band wouldn't squeeze and that it would fit comfortably. Well, just before he measured I took a deep breath—so this band is really very roomy. I can slip out of it any time I want to. I do sometimes, on warm evenings. Look here—I'll exhale!"

Arab's body became so slim as he breathed out that he almost slipped out of his metal band.

"Oh! Oh! Breathe in again. Quick!" said the old horse, in a panic, as he threw a worried glance at Mr. Bill and Mr. Timothy.

But fortunately they were talking about yesterday's baseball scores and they had not noticed. When Arab had again adjusted himself and again filled his band as he properly should, the old coach horse let out a sigh of relief.

"Please don't do that again," he said as he shook away the drops of perspiration that had gathered on his bony forehead. "No more tricks, please, or this matter's closed right now."

Arab hung his head from his fine curved neck.

"I might have spoken too harshly," said the coach horse. "But this is a serious matter and we must deal seriously with it. Frankly I'm just as anxious as you are for your day of freedom—and, I must confess, for my own sake as well."

Arab looked up again.

"Yes, for my own sake," continued the coach horse. "This day of freedom for you will be a day of rest for me. It will give me a chance to catch up with some sleep and putter around my stall doing a lot of things I've always wanted to do. Trotting around the hard city pavement might be an adventure for you, but for me it's just the same old grind. I'm not blaming anyone. Mr. Bill is a kind master. There's nothing he expects from me that he'd not do himself. He feeds me the same as he does his own family. I'm one of the family, so to

speak. We all have oatmeal porridge for breakfast, salad for lunch—and in the evening, since I don't like roast beef (I let them know that from the first), I have the finest hay available."

Arab kept quiet for fear of offending the old coach horse again. He looked as sympathetic as he could, hoping his day of freedom was not completely lost. After a moment the coach horse went on.

"Yes, Mr. Bill treats me right. But he has a large family and responsibilities. He never takes a day off, so neither do I. But, after all, I am a bachelor."

Arab nodded.

"Look here, Young One," said the coach horse after a pause. "Let's cheer up about this thing. Now here's my plan, and pay strict attention."

His plan was simple indeed. Anyone could have followed his careful instructions. Arab was to bide his time, and on a certain day the old coach horse would signal him in the morning to be ready to start as the six-o'clock whistle was blowing.

They would wait until the summer was over.

"We wouldn't want to disappoint the children," said the old horse. "We'll pick a cold cloudy day when they're all at school and we're sure they will not come to the park. You know, they'd miss you if you weren't here."

"Yes," said Arab doubtfully, remembering those boys who kicked at his ribs as they played cowboys and Indians on his back. "Well, then, that's what we'll do," said the coach horse.

"Pick a nice cold day in the late fall when it gets dark early. After Mr. Timothy locks up the merry-go-round, you slip out of your metal band as you showed me."

"Like this?" said Arab, with a twinkle in his eye as he slowly began to breathe out.

"That will do—now don't do that again. Please. All right —you slip out of your band as the six-o'clock whistle blows, jump the iron fence that goes round the merry-go-round. You can easily do it, the way you've been hopping around."

"Even if it were higher," said proud Arab.

"Mmm, yes," said the coach horse. "Now where was I? Yes, you jump the fence and head right down this road. I believe in about five minutes you should reach the edge of the park. I've done it in twenty myself, pulling this coach, old as I am. You should do it in five, since you have only your own weight to carry and you're a few years younger."

"Guess I could do it in three."

"No more interruptions, please. Now listen carefully. This is important. At the edge of the park you turn left. Remember

25

that—left, not right. Do you know your left from your right?"

"Of course," said Arab, waving his left hoof in the air.

"You're right—that's left. There are some young ones who don't. After you turn, go along the street that borders the park —just half a block. Cross over when the traffic light turns red, and then, if you've followed my instructions carefully, you should be at the mouth of our alley. Look sharp, for it's very narrow—just wide enough for our coach wheels. Very well. Trot on tiptoes down our alley to the end, and you come to my stable. Quietly, remember, because Mr. Bill and his family live above my stall. Now you should be there about ten after six. The Bill family will be eating their supper, and I believe I should just about be finishing mine. Of course you

26

will have had your supper before you started out."

"No, I won't," said Arab.

"No?"

Arab laughed. "Don't worry, Old One. I don't expect you to feed me. We merry-go-rounders never eat. Good Mr. Timothy rubs us down with oil and paints over the chips some children kick into our sides now and then. That's all we need."

"Indeed?" said the coach horse as a worrisome thought wrinkled his brow.

He remembered how Mr. Bill complained about the high cost of oats and hay, and realized there was some risk for him in this venture. What if Mr. Bill discovered them? What if he learned he could have a fine young horse made of wonder wood pull the coach all day long, year in and year out, for nothing more than an occasional rub of oil and a dab of paint now and then?

"Now, Young One, remember—I'm just letting you have my job for one night and a day. That's all. It's not permanent."

Arab vowed he would not attempt to take the coach job forever. Then the old coach horse had Arab repeat his instructions back, to be sure he knew every detail of the plan as far as he had gone.

"Good," said the coach horse. "You have a remarkable memory. Now when the day comes we'll arrange the details of what must follow. Good-by. Here comes Mr. Bill."

"Go in peace," said Arab.

3. The Day of Days

ARAB'S HEART WAS SO FULL of happiness he felt it would burst for joy. Gaily he pranced, swiftly he whirled (sometimes nudging the horse in front of him on the merry-go-round to go faster), and he even developed a sideward rock to add excitement to the rides he gave the children. If the children had thought Arab was the finest horse on the merry-go-round before he learned the old coach horse's plan, from that day on they decided he was even finer—that he was the best in the world!

They admired him so that all the way home from the park

the big boys would prance, dance, and whirl as they sang, "Look, here's how Arab goes. See, this is the way he jumps round and round and up and down."

And the little girls would clap their hands in glee because the boys were so funny and looked so little as Arab really looked.

Finally summer was over. All the children went back to school—all the children, that is, except those who were too little and had to be held on the merry-go-round even though they were strapped to the horses.

The leaves of the trees around the merry-go-round changed from bright green to soft yellow and orange. Fewer and fewer children came to the park in the afternoon. They had to do their homework. The days became shorter and colder. Then at last the leaves turned to a deep, deep red and, one by one, fell off the trees and fluttered to the ground.

Yes, summer was gone and fall had come.

On a cold gray morning the old coach horse trotted briskly up the road. His breath steamed from his mouth in a long white plume, his hoofs struck sparks on the road, and there was a purposeful gleam in his eye. All the way from the stable Mr. Bill had pulled at the reins, trying to keep him from wasting his strength. After all there was no sense using up so much energy when there were no customers in the coach. But there was no holding the old coach horse.

Mr. Bill said to Mr. Timothy, when they pulled up at the merry-go-round, that he couldn't imagine what had got into

29

the Old One. Perhaps that last bag of oats had too many vitamins in it.

They didn't know, but young Arab did. He knew why the coach horse had dashed through the park to get to the merry-go-round *that* morning. This was the day of days. Arab's day of freedom.

"Tell me. Oh, please tell me, Old One, that this is the day," Arab hoarsely whispered over the iron fence.

The old coach horse puffed and snorted a minute or two as he rolled his eyes toward Arab.

"Let me catch my breath," he gasped. "I shouldn't have run like that. It brings on my asthma."

"But tell me. Just nod your head if you can't talk. Is it or isn't it?"

The old horse nodded. "Yes, it is. I'm all right now. It was just my asthma. Comes the damp weather . . ."

Arab waited as politely as he could until the old coach horse had told of his asthma, rheumatism, colds, chilblains, and all the other afflictions that bothered him in the fall—and went on to tell of the measures he took to cure himself.

"Well, I put my forehoofs in a fine bucket of hot water and then . . ."

But Arab wasn't listening. His eyes looked off through the leafless branches, and a blissful grin lit up his dark slender face.

"You're not paying attention," said the coach horse.

"I am," said Arab. "You were saying you put your fore-hoofs in a hot bucket."

"I said that ten minutes ago. Right now I merely asked you to repeat my instructions—that's all. Of course, if you've changed your mind about the whole thing—"

"Oh! No, no," Arab hurried to assure him.

Then he quickly rattled off the list of instructions the coach horse had repeated almost every day for the past two months. He missed up only on the turn.

"It's left," said the coach horse sternly. "Left, remember. That's important. If you turn right, you'll be lost forever. You must turn left. You're always making that mistake. Here now—if you had two apples and you ate one, what would you have left? That's it. Left."

"I don't eat apples," said Arab.

"Never mind that. Remember it's left. As you leave the park, turn left. Here comes Mr. Bill again with his coat unbuttoned—he'll catch his death. Here we go again. Remember it's left. . . . Good-by, Young One. Good luck."

Arab's heart was too full to talk. He just waved farewell with his left hoof and set the whole merry-go-round atremble. And all through the day Arab quivered with such eagerness to be off that Mr. Timothy kept tinkering with the machinery trying to find out why his merry-go-round shook so. It seemed he'd never go home that afternoon. But as the light faded and the rain began to drizzle down he finally quit.

Arab heard him murmuring that he'd have to have an expert mechanic look at that flywheel before the spring came round again.

"Maybe," Mr. Timothy said to himself, "the old merry-go-round is falling apart. It may not be safe for the children."

But at last he bundled himself up, opened his umbrella, locked the gate, and was gone.

Slowly, carefully, noiselessly, Arab breathed out. The metal band was loose around his chest. Quickly he slipped out of it and stood tense in the gathering darkness waiting for the six-o'clock whistle. Since there was no one along the road that led to the merry-go-round, he tried a practice jump over the fence. He cleared it easily and jumped back and forth a few times.

"Good!" he said to himself. "I knew I could do it. All right now. Blow, Whistle, blow!"

Time moved so slowly in the darkness! Arab was tempted to clear the fence and race off to the coach horse's stable before the arranged signal. It was so hard to wait.

Suddenly there it was. Toot-toot-toot—the six-o'clock whistle!

He sailed through the air and landed on the slippery road in a scramble. Then, laughing at his clumsiness, he gathered himself together and fairly flew around the bend of the road that led to the edge of the park.

Arab was free!

4. How Arab Crossed the Park

Yes, Arab was free!

He had whirled around the bend in the road with the speed of the wind and then . . .

What happened? He didn't know! He found himself lying at the foot of a big fat tree. Now for the first time Arab understood what some little girls meant when they giggled they were dizzy after just two rides on the merry-go-round. Everything whirled around him and he felt very dizzy indeed. The first time in history that a merry-go-round horse became dizzy! Slowly he looked around. He was still on the road to the edge of the park. The tree under which he was lying was one of those tremendous elms whose branches stretch across the broad road.

"I must have been going too fast," said Arab to himself. "Guess I crashed up against this tree trunk. Well, no damage done. Just a few chips of paint off my chest. It's a good thing wonder wood can't break or splinter."

He carefully arose. The cold rain had covered the broad road with a sheet of ice and the bright blue lights from the lampposts spotted along the way were reflected in its glittering surface.

"Ah," he said, "so that's what it was—ice. I must have skidded."

He started off again, not at his top speed—just about half. Round and round and up and down he went. Again he found himself on the side of the road instead of the center he'd been aiming at.

Arab stood firm in the gutter that ran along the road and tried to figure it out.

"Now, what can be the matter?"

Then, in one of those flashes of clear thinking that sometimes come to us all, he understood—Arab discovered he could not go straight forward, and he could not turn left. Only right! But the road ahead curved gently to the *left!*

All through the summer he'd been speeding around the merry-go-round turning to the right. Always to the right. Mr. Timothy had set up all the horses on the merry-go-round so they would go that way. He thought it would do the children good to learn early in life that traffic always keeps to the right.

"It's a turn-right habit," said Arab. "That's what it is! Maybe that's the reason I kept forgetting the Old One's instructions to turn to the left. I always thought right, because we all turned right. That's what it is—just a habit."

Arab didn't worry whether it was a good habit or a bad habit, like those little boys had who scuffed their shoes in the ground as they waited for their turn to ride. Some little girls untied and retied their hair ribbons as they waited in line, and others chewed their fingernails—the worst habit of all.

"Now that I know what it is, I can cure it easily," thought Arab. "Let me see—right is not right. Right is not might. Turn left—all right. Well, here goes."

And off he went. Very slowly this time. Quarter speed— as when the merry-go-round is just starting up. But try as he might, and though he kept chanting to himself, "Right is not right. Left is right," Arab still turned to the right.

He impatiently stamped his hoofs.

"I'll break that habit," he said grimly, "if it's the last thing I do."

Then the thought struck him and he remembered his date with the old coach horse.

"Glory me," he said. "What time can it be? How long have I lain under this tree I bumped into? How long have I spent getting nowhere on this icy road? I'd better think of the

quickest way to get to the Old One's stable—and leave this habit-breaking for some other time."

Arab tried many, many ways of going along that road—with no better success. He tried going even slower—hardly moving. He tried going faster. He even tried going backwards! But always he turned to the right, ending up in the same place under the same fat elm tree.

Arab looked toward the brightly lit street at the edge of the park. His throat was as dry as splinters. If he could have cried, he would have.

"Oh, stop this nonsense," he said to himself. "And think!"

Finally he decided, since he knew where he wanted to go, he must get there in his own way.

So, instead of continuing along the road as the coach horse had instructed him, Arab set his course directly for the lighted street. He went round and round and up and down, whirling in great big loops right across the road over the wide frozen lawns with their ice-covered "Keep off the Grass" signs, through the zoo, across some more roads and lawns. And quicker than I can tell it he arrived at the stone wall that surrounds the park. Lightly he hopped over the wall—and there he was in the street.

He squinted through the raindrops, and directly across the broad street he saw a narrow dark passage between two buildings.

"That must be the Old One's alley," said Arab hopefully.

And, strange to say, it was!

Arab waited until the traffic light turned red, and then in two fine large right loops he whirled round and round and up and down—and he was safely across the broad streets, and was standing at the entrance to the coach horse's alley.

"There now," said Arab, with a sigh of relief. "I did it!"

Fortunately no one had seen Arab whirling madly across the park. There was no one going along the street as he had hopped over the wall and gone across the street in the strange way he moved. I'm sure that if anyone had been he'd have gone to bed promptly, believing he had caught something and was seeing things because of a high fever. And well he might have (gone to bed I mean), for it was a bitter cold night and now the rain that had started as a drizzle was really coming down. The big drops froze as soon as they splashed on the ground. Ice covered everything.

There were not even any policemen or postmen out and around as they always are no matter what the weather. It was suppertime and they too must eat nourishing food to carry on their work.

Just for a moment or two Arab stood and looked along the

street and up at the tall buildings with their thousands of windows twinkling their red and yellow and blue lights through the raindrops.

"Like stars they are," said Arab, with a happy sigh. "Yes, this Bagdad of the West is very beautiful."

Then, as he again remembered his waiting friend, he chuckled to himself, "Enough of this star-gazing, young Arab. Your adventure is just beginning and you'd better move on before your foolish hoofs are frozen into this quickly gathering ice, and it will all end right here."

Arab looked down the dark alley and saw a glow of light from some windows at the far end.

"Yes, that is my friend's stable. I can smell the fragrant hay he eats for supper."

Arab's nostrils were very sensitive.

"Yes, my friend waits for me," he sang softly as he turned into the alley—luckily a right turn—and he hummed as he went on:

"My friend waits for me beneath the desert stars—Abdul,
    Abdul.
 In the sweet-scented breeze the camels sing—Allul, Allul."

And to the tune of that fine Arabian song, which he had just remembered, he quietly trotted on tiptoes down the alley to the coach horse's door.

5. Arab in Disguise

ARAB PUSHED THE STABLE DOOR OPEN. In a low happy voice he greeted the old coach horse.

"Salaam, Old One."

"Salaam, alaykoum—and shut the door," was the coach horse's cold response.

Arab with a gay flip of his hind leg slammed the door shut.

"Old One," he said, "do you know 'The Song of the Dark Shepherd'? It's by one of the younger poets. It goes, 'My friend waits' . . ."

"Shush," hissed the coach horse angrily. "And, please, stop

that humming. You'll ruin everything."

Arab was quiet. His face had become sober, but the song went on inside of him.

"Slamming doors . . . humming songs," grumbled the coach horse. "We'll be ruined if Mr. Bill comes down before you're properly disguised. And you're late. We'll hardly have time for—"

"You did say ten after six. Remember?" said Arab anxiously. He hoped he would not have to explain why he was late.

"Well, you can plainly see," snapped the coach horse, "it's half past the hour now. There—look at my clock on the wall."

"Why, you do have a clock!" said Arab, and he continued looking around the stable with murmurs of admiration for everything. "By the Beard of the Prophet! This is truly the tent of a sheik, not a stable."

"Yes, it's comfortable," murmured the flattered coach horse. "It's snug, well equipped—electric lights, running water, oil-stove heater, and—look there—I have a telephone." He proudly pointed his hoof to a dark object hung alongside the clock.

"No! Really?" said Arab. "Indeed you do have a telephone. I can see it. I never heard of anything like that. A stable with a telephone."

"Well, yes, it is unusual," said the coach horse modestly—by now he had completely forgotten he'd been angry with the tardy Arab—"since this is a one-horse stable. Of course they

43

do have telephones in the large crowded livery stables, but it is rare to have a telephone for one horse. And it's *unlisted!*"

"Unlisted? My, my!" said Arab, widening his eyes at that.

"Yes," said the coach horse as he gave Arab a sidelong glance. He suspected (correctly) that Arab had no idea what an unlisted telephone was.

There were many things Arab knew about the city even though he had not seen much more than the clump of trees that surrounded the merry-go-round. And how did he learn so much about all the things we see and use every day, such as traffic lights, clocks, telephones, books, knitting needles, hockey sticks, and so on? The children had taught him!

As they waited in line at the merry-go-round they talked to one another about everything, and Arab listened carefully. He did have a remarkable memory. He never forgot a thing. In truth, listening and remembering, both here and abroad he had learned a number of languages besides Horse Arabic. He understood (though he could not speak) Dutch, French, English, and a little Swedish. That last he had learned on the ship coming over. But never had he heard any of the children or anyone else talk of an unlisted telephone.

"Of course it's very special," the old coach horse went on, with a careless wave of his hoof. "Our telephone number is private. It's not listed in the regular telephone books, so we are never bothered with wrong numbers or with boys and girls just calling up for fun—pretending they're somebody else."

44

"I see." Arab nodded an understanding head and tucked this new bit of knowledge away in his memory, along with all the other things he had learned.

"The only people who know this telephone number are our special customers. It's only for business and not for friendly conversation, so I'm sorry I can't tell it to you."

Arab nodded again. "Everything is very special," he said admiringly.

"Yes," said the coach horse, looking around the stable with a pleased smile. "Yes, indeed. Small, snug, but very special."

There was a sound of chairs being scraped along the floor overhead.

"Oh my! They're getting up from the table already, and we've stood here chattering. Mr. Bill might be down any minute now for our after-supper calls. We'll have to disguise you quickly. Now let me see—here, try on this bridle for size. I see you've left yours at home."

In the excitement of his escape from the merry-go-round Arab had lost his bridle and saddle. He wondered where, as he slipped into the coach horse's second-best bridle and harness.

"Fits you perfectly," said the coach horse. "Maybe a tuck here in the back—and we might do something with that shoulder strap. But we haven't time right now. Then—here's this Scotch plaid blanket coat. Just slip into it. . . . Yes, that looks as if it were made for you. Please be careful with it. The lining tears so easily."

Arab felt strangely stiff all dressed up. He had never worn so many trappings before. But he still was not disguised enough to suit the old coach horse.

"Let's see. What else can we do?" said the coach horse as he studied his face in the gold-framed mirror that hung over his feedbox. "You know we do look alike—I suppose being Arabian and all. Oh! Oh! I forgot this hat. It's a summer hat —but I wear it all the time, even indoors to protect me from drafts. Better put it on too. No one would believe you were I unless you wore it."

He rubbed his head against one of the stable posts, and the weather-beaten old straw hat tumbled to the floor. Arab picked

it up by slipping his narrow muzzle through the strap, and then tossed the hat onto his head.

"Wear it straight," said the coach horse. "I always do. Now back into the shafts—I'll snap on your straps."

Arab did as he was directed. The coach horse with a few quick nibbles snapped the harness to the shafts and to the coach's whippletree. Then he studied Arab from various angles.

"There you are. The very image of me except for one detail. Your complexion—you're quite a bit darker than I am. Did Mr. Timothy wash your face this morning? Never mind. I have an idea."

The coach horse picked up a few long wisps of hay, dipped them into the white dust of his feedbox, and brushed over Arab's face lightly. Then he stepped back and looked at Arab with one eye almost closed.

"Perfect!" said the coach horse. "Absolutely perfect! My own mother couldn't tell us apart."

With some difficulty Arab squinted through the slits of his blinders and saw himself reflected in the mirror over the feedbox. "Mine could," he thought, but he didn't say anything.

"There you are, Young One. You're all ready," said the coach horse, and after a glance at the clock he busily pushed together a fine soft bed of dry straw on the floor of his stall. "Any minute now," he said. "Any minute Mr. Bill will be finishing his after-supper pipe, and come down. I'll give you

48

your last instruction after I stretch out."

The coach horse, with a luxurious sigh, settled down to his bed of straw. He made a few corrections—a little more straw under his withers, a little less under his head. Then he covered himself with a thick blanket of straw. Only his big bony head was visible. Blissfully he closed his eyes and for a moment there was silence in the stable.

"Ah-h," he said. "This feels good. I'm going to enjoy your day of freedom, Young One."

Again there was a sound of a chair scraping the floor overhead—only one this time. The coach horse's eyes flew open.

"Listen sharp now," he said. "That means Mr. Bill's finished his second cup of tea and lit up his pipe again. He should be down here in a moment. You still look all right . . . but

relax a little. Don't stand so stiffly. I never do. One more thing —please kick some straw over my head, so you can see none of me."

Arab followed his instructions.

"That's fine. Just tuck a little more back of my head. . . . And if it's not too much trouble would you mind reaching over and dropping a few mouthfuls of that fresh hay— There, that over in the corner—just drop it down here in front of me, so I won't have to get all undone in the early morning to get at it. For once I'll enjoy breakfast in bed."

That was more difficult, but Arab managed in spite of being hitched to the coach.

Aside from one large eye that peeped out from the hill of straw, the old coach horse was gone from the face of the earth. That eye twinkled as his voice came through the straw.

"Thank you. For once now I'll have breakfast in bed," and as the sound of heavy footsteps sounded overhead the coach horse's eye disappeared. One last message came from the pile of straw: "Good night, Young One. Good luck. Try not to wake me when you come in."

Arab could hear Mr. Bill climbing down the stairs now. Under his breath he whispered, "Allah, Allah, ishm Allah!"

That was a little prayer.

6. Mr. Bill Bumps His Head

MR. BILL CLUMPED DOWN THE STAIRS briskly buttoning his greatcoat. He gave Arab an absent-minded pat on the back and murmured that he was a good old horse.

"Yes, there aren't many horses who would have the sense to harness themselves up and get ready for their jobs. You're a lot of help, Old Horse."

The tobacco smoke from his pipe mixed with the scent of the hay. Arab's delicate nostrils sniffed the fragrance. Mr. Bill hoped he was not catching cold. He stood there sucking his pipe as he looked down at Arab's hoofs for a long, long minute.

Arab began to fidget. Could it be that Mr. Bill saw through his disguise?

B-r-r-r went the telephone. Arab jumped with surprise. He'd never heard the sharp ring of a telephone bell before.

"Easy, Old Boy," muttered Mr. Bill as he clumped by to answer the impatient ringing. "I'm coming. I'm coming."

Out of the corner of his eye Arab saw the hill of straw twitching nervously.

" 'Ello. Mr. Bill speaking," said Mr. Bill. "Who? Mr. Gorman? Oh yes, Mr. Gorman. Yes, sir. Yes? Yes, we could. Let me see. We could—that is, if it would not take longer than a half-hour. It's almost time for Mrs. Worthington's ride to the pigeon roost. . . . No-o-o, I'm sorry I couldn't postpone it. Sure, I know it's a bitter-cold night, but Mrs. Worthington feeds the pigeons no matter what the weather is. She's faithful to her pigeons, she is. All right, then, I'll start out right now. We'll meet you in front of Mrs. Worthington's hotel at the corner of the park. . . . 'By."

Mr. Bill slammed the receiver on its hook and came back to Arab muttering angrily.

"Nonsense! Of all the foolish nonsense. Wants to practice for the parade on a night like this. Ach!"

Mr. Bill was so exasperated with Mr. Gorman's telephone call he had to return twice to pick up things he'd forgotten after he had led Arab to the stable door. Once to get his rubbers —then again to pluck his long whip out of the umbrella

52

stand. The whip was one of those long shiny leather-bound sticks of a whip—the kind that is topped with a little flick of braided cord and a tassel. It was quite a bit taller than stocky Mr. Bill and looked very pretty with a pink ribbon tied in a large bow near the top. Like a long-stemmed hibiscus flower, thought Arab, and he was tempted to sing the song "The hibiscus flower by the river's brim."

Old Coach Horse had once told Arab that Mr. Bill never used the whip. It was against his principles and, besides, using it would fray the ribbon. Those ribbons were laundered as often as Mr. Bill's shirts.

After a few more false starts they were on their way.

Mr. Bill threw open the stable door, looked up at the dark wet sky, and shook his head.

" 'Tain't a fit night for man nor beast," he muttered. "But we're in the public service, Old Horse. We have our duty to perform."

So saying, with one hand grasping Arab's bridle and the other his long whip, he bent his head and led Arab down the narrow alley to the street.

The stiff shafts of the coach kept Arab from turning quickly to the right as was his habit. Coming up the alley, he had trotted along the wall and scraped off more than a little paint as he kept turning right into the unyielding bricks.

Just as they reached the street Mr. Bill stopped and faced Arab.

53

"Old Horse," he said, "what are you bounding up and down for?"

Naturally Arab said nothing since he could only understand English. He couldn't speak it.

"Must be those oats. . . . Gawsh! Look at there. I forgot to lock the stable door—that Mr. Gorman and his telephoning!"

And Mr. Bill ducked his head under Arab's neck to start back to the stable. He hadn't ducked down far enough and he bumped his head just a little against Arab's throat. Clunk!

Well, did you ever bump your head even just a little bump against an iron bar? Then you can imagine how Mr. Bill felt. For wonder wood, though it is light and lively, is as hard as iron, so even a little bump hurts.

"Gawsh!" said Mr. Bill, rubbing his forehead. "Old Horse, you're getting bonier than ever. We'll have to fatten you up a bit. I think we'll have to mix some cod-liver oil in your breakfast porridge and less of those jumpy oats."

Arab hoped the coach horse liked cod-liver oil in his porridge.

Now, since the coach filled the alley, Mr. Bill had to squeeze through the narrow space between Arab and the brick wall, then climb over the coach to go back and lock the stable door. And he had to go through the same process to get back to Arab's head.

He was not in a very good mood and he grumbled as he led Arab out of the alley with no further mishap. Fortunately the turn out into the street was a right one. Mr. Bill muttered there was no sense climbing up on his coach seat to travel just half a block to the corner of the park. He led Arab along the icy street.

Now the rain had again become only a drizzle.

Arab tried hard to keep from going up and down and round and round to the right. He didn't have to try too hard, since Mr. Bill walked so slowly on the icy street. Anyway Mr. Bill blamed the strong wind, the icy pavements, and the oats for

the zigzag bumpy passage he and Arab made to the corner of the park.

There were four winter coaches like Mr. Bill's coach lined up along the curb across the street from Mrs. Worthington's hotel. And all the blanketed coach horses standing there with their heads drooping looked very much like Mr. Bill's old coach horse.

"Ah, more Arabians," said Arab to himself. He nickered a "Salaam" to each as he passed.

Two of them turned their old heads and asked, "What?" The third horse said, "Never heard of him." And the fourth was either asleep or stone deaf. He said nothing.

Their masters, the coachmen, were gathered around a fire that blazed from a rusty iron barrel on the sidewalk. Mr. Bill

had a little trouble getting Arab and his coach in place at the end of the line. A gust of wind helped push the coach wheels over to the curb. Then Mr. Bill joined the group around the fire.

" 'Ullo, Mr. Bill."

"Evenin', Bill."

"Hiya, Bill."

"Hi."

Mr. Bill answered them all with one wave of his hand.

"Good evening, men."

"What's good about it?" asked one of the coachmen.

"You're right," said Mr. Bill. "It's horrible weather."

7. Arab is a Saddle Horse

ARAB WAS VERY HAPPY standing at the end of the line. Anything could happen now. Indeed something was due to happen right away! Mr. Gorman! Arab didn't know where Mr. Gorman wanted to go, but wherever it was it was bound to be interesting. Had not Mr. Bill angrily grumbled something about practicing for a parade? That's what Mr. Gorman had telephoned he wanted to do. Well, where do parades usually march? Usually? Always! Along the best, broadest, longest, most important street of any city. Everyone knows that.

And Arab, Mr. Bill, and Mr. Gorman very probably would take a quick canter along those streets where the parade was going to march, so that Mr. Gorman would know the route of the parade by heart and would not have to look at the map as the parade marched along. He hoped Mr. Gorman would hurry along.

Mr. Bill had been telling the other coachmen about Mr. Gorman's telephone call. Arab, busy with his own thoughts, hadn't been paying attention at first, but after he heard Mr. Gorman's name mentioned he listened carefully.

" 'Mr. Gorman,' says I," said Mr. Bill, " 'I am sorry I won't postpone Mrs. Worthington's ride for a million. No, sir,' says I, 'that kind old lady's worth her weight in gold.' "

That wasn't the way Arab remembered Mr. Bill's part of the conversation. Maybe that's what Mr. Bill wished he'd said, for all the coachmen nodded their heads solemnly and mumbled.

"That she is. Yes, sir, that little lady's worth a ton."

"Mind you—I've nothing against Mr. Gorman. He's one of my regular customers, and my horse and coach and myself are at his service—"

Then one coachman, the only one who did not read the newspaper—only books—asked what Mr. Gorman's parade was about. All the others were amazed. Why, it was the talk of the town! The most important day since school opened.

Mr. Bill, choosing his words very carefully, as one does when one is talking to a very simple-minded person, told him about it. Mr. Gorman was *the* Mr. Gorman. The famous toyshop man. He owned the Gorman Toyshops—they were all over the city. Of course everyone had seen his advertisements in the newspapers, on the trolleys, and on the billboards.

GORMAN'S TOYS

FOR

GIRLS AND BOYS

Well, tomorrow Mr. Gorman planned to open the new toyshop—the biggest in the world. The Forty-story Toyshop that was being built just a block from where the coachmen stood. Hadn't the book-reading coachman seen that big building going up? He nodded he had, but he thought it was a new garage. Well, it wasn't. It's the big Gorman Toyshop.

Tomorrow after school Mr. Gorman would lead the biggest, finest parade anyone had ever seen up the avenue and around the city and to the door of his Forty-story Toyshop. There would be the biggest bands, biggest balloons, biggest floats, biggest everything that befits the biggest toyshop in the world.

"A big event," the book-reading coachman finally admitted.

And as he said that a large shiny automobile drove up and stopped in the darkness a few yards away from Arab's coach. A little butterball of a man climbed out. He was carrying a large saddle with both hands.

It was Mr. Gorman!

He hissed toward the group of coachmen.

"Ps-s-s-t, Mr. Bill."

Mr. Bill left the group around the fire.

61

"Good evening, Mr. Bill. Here I am on the dot." He spoke in a squeaky high-pitched voice.

"Evening, Mr. Gorman. What's that you have? A saddle? What for?"

"Not so loud, Mr. Bill," whispered Mr. Gorman. "I brought it along to practice on."

"Why?"

"To lead the parade as I told you."

"Sorry, Mr. Gorman," said the puzzled Mr. Bill. "I still don't understand. I thought you were leading the parade in a coach, all decked out with flags and bunting on it—and the Mayor in it. At least, so this evening's paper said."

"The Mayor won't be able to come. He's got a cold and I'd look rather silly sitting in a coach alone, and—well, it's been so many years since I rode a horse I thought if I practiced a little tonight—"

"Now, now. See here, Mr. Gorman, I'd be happy to help you out—but I'm running a coaching business, not a riding academy."

Mr. Gorman had become pinker and pinker with embarrassment and his voice had developed a tremble.

Finally Mr. Bill agreed to take Arab out of his shafts for Mr. Gorman to practice riding on. He would hate to have the parade held up tomorrow while everyone waited for the leader of the parade to climb back on his horse every time he fell off. And he'd charge Mr. Gorman only half price for the half-hour, since the coach was not being used.

They unhitched Arab and led him out of his shafts.

There was some difficulty strapping Mr. Gorman's saddle over and around the bulky Scotch-plaid blanket coat Arab wore. But that's the only way Mr. Gorman could hire his horse, Mr. Bill insisted. He'd not have his old horse catching cold on this nasty night.

It was a great relief to Arab the argument ended that way. For if Mr. Gorman had had his way and Arab's blanket coat had been taken off they surely would have seen through his disguise. Then goodness knows what might have happened.

Mr. Gorman led Arab around the curb into the dimlit park (a right turn) so that he could climb up on a stone and then get up on Arab's back. He climbed down once to shorten the stirrup straps to fit his short legs. At last he was satisfied and sat straight on Arab's back, holding the reins.

"Now, Old Horse. We're ready," he said. "Now just

imagine a lot of people . . . flags waving . . . the band begins playing. . . . One, two . . . One, two . . . March! Ta-ta-tra. Ta-ta-tra."

And he kicked Arab in the ribs!

That was a mistake. Had he been riding Mr. Bill's plodding old coach horse that kick in the ribs would have sent him shuffling along at his top speed, which was not much faster than most people walk. But to Arab, who had a stubborn streak in his nature, the kick in the ribs meant not top speed. On the contrary, it meant "I won't move a step."

Mr. Gorman slapped the reins, bounced up and down—but to no avail. Arab would not budge an inch!

Finally Mr. Gorman said, "Please, Horse, go—ta-ta-tra."

"That's better," said Arab to himself, and off he went.

Round and round . . . Up and down . . . Round and round . . . and up and down! He whirled in big swirling loops across the road, over the lawn, and back around to the road, and . . . Round and round again!

Mr. Gorman held onto the reins for dear life as he was bounced and banged around on Arab's hard back. He lost hold of one rein and it slapped against Arab's neck.

"S-o-o! You want me to do better?" said Arab to himself. "Kicks in the rib—slaps on the neck. All right, little man. Here we go."

Faster and faster he went. Higher and harder bounced poor Mr. Gorman.

Even the thickness of his saddle and Coach Horse's blanket coat could not soften the bump every time he landed on Arab's ironlike back. He wasn't strapped onto his seat as all the boys and girls had been who rode Arab on the merry-go-round.

"Dear me!" gasped the amazed Mr. Gorman. "What have we here?"

The other rein was shaken from Mr. Gorman's hand. He made a wild grab for Arab's neck and clung on for a breathless moment.

"He likes it," thought Arab, and he went even faster.

When Mr. Gorman could finally catch his breath he shouted, "Whoa! Please, whoa!"

Arab stood stock-still!

He had stopped so suddenly Mr. Gorman was thrown head over heels. And he zoomed off into space like a shooting star! He landed with a great CRASH and a BANG right in the middle of the boxwood hedge across the road!

Quietly, politely, Arab waited until Mr. Gorman climbed out of the hedge and painfully limped across the road.

"That proves it," said Mr. Gorman, gathering up the reins and preparing to mount again. "That proves it. I do need practice."

How many times did Mr. Gorman remount? How many more times was he whirled, bounced, and thrown (always into the boxwood hedge) in that half-hour? I don't know. And I'm sure Arab lost count. But off he'd go into the hedge, and out he'd climb—and be thrown back in again and again! Out he came and back he went.

When his half-hour was up, Mr. Gorman staggered out of the park and led Arab back to Mr. Bill's coach.

"How did it go?" asked Mr. Bill. "Did you get a lot of practice in?"

"Yes," said Mr. Gorman in a weak voice. "I did have quite a little practice on the turns and curves, but not enough on the straightaway. I'll lead the parade in my automobile."

Then as he turned to go he added, "Please charge it, Mr. Bill. Good night," and he quickly drove away in his long shiny automobile.

" 'Night, Mr. Gorman. . . . Now what could he have meant by that talk about turns, curves, and all that?" mumbled Mr. Bill as he dragged out his little black book to jot down: "October 30. Mr. Gorman—one half-hour horse without coach, 75 cents."

That's the way he did his bookkeeping. Mr. Bill sent out bills to all his customers on the first of the month.

While Mr. Bill was hitching Arab back onto the coach, the doorman in front of Mrs. Worthington's hotel blew his whistle. Three shrill blasts.

"There's our signal, Old Horse," said Mr. Bill. "Mrs. Worthington's coming down. O.K.," he shouted across the street. "We heard you. We'll be there in a minute."

68

8. Nut Cake and Pigeon Slippers

GENTLE MRS. WORTHINGTON was already down, and waiting patiently under the big umbrella the doorman held over her head, by the time Mr. Bill had climbed up on his coach seat. He drove Arab across the wide street in a large right turn.

"Good thing that was my kind of turn," said Arab to himself. "And it's lucky too—we're going to turn right into the park. Too bad I didn't think of it—I could have practiced left turns during Mr. Gorman's half-hour."

"Faithful Mr. William," said Mrs. Worthington as the doorman helped her into the coach.

She was a refined old lady who never used nicknames. Mr. Bill liked her calling him Mr. William.

"You're the faithful one, Mrs. Worthington," said Mr. Bill, doffing his hat. "Faithful to your pigeons. Come fine weather or foul."

"The dear pigeons," said Mrs. Worthington sadly. "My dear, dear pigeons. If I did not bring them this bag of cake crumbs every evening—how could they sleep through the night?"

"Yes, ma'am," said Mr. Bill, picking up his reins. "Giddyap, Old Horse."

"Everyone needs a snack before going to bed," said Mrs. Worthington. "Even pigeons. But no one seems to think of that."

"You do," said Mr. Bill.

"Ah yes," said Mrs. Worthington. "I'd toss and turn all night on my goose-feather bed if I thought those poor little waifs had gone to roost with their dear little stomachs empty."

"You've a kind heart," said Mr. Bill.

"It's only my nature," replied Mrs. Worthington.

Arab had turned slowly right into the park, and had made just two large right round-and-round loops on the broad road during Mrs. Worthington's and Mr. Bill's conversation. Arab had moved so slowly and his up-and-down movement had been so gentle that neither Mr. Bill, looking back into the coach, nor Mrs. Worthington had noticed it.

"Here! Here, Old Horse," said Mr. Bill as he turned about in his seat. "Let's get on with it. It's the pigeons' going-to-bed snack we're bringing 'em, not their breakfast." And he slapped the reins gently on Arab's back.

"Ah me," said Arab to himself. "Well, here we go. Hold onto your hats, everybody."

And away he went. Up and down. Round and round, in his big whirling loops! Across the roads! Over the hedges! Over the lawns. . . .

The coach whipped out in back of him like the tail of a kite. Mrs. Worthington bounced around in the coach like a dry pea in a pod. Mr. Bill almost swallowed his pipe in surprise.

Presto! They had arrived in a whirlwind of twigs and rain-drops at the pigeon roost!

Arab stopped short and stood quietly.

"Gosh," said Mr. Bill, and he blinked.

For a moment he was dazed! He didn't know what to think. The awakened pigeons, who had flown up into the night in a cloud of flapping wings, soon settled back to their roost with little cooing noises. But they always acted that way when the coach arrived, even on ordinary nights.

"I must have fallen asleep," mumbled Mr. Bill.

He knew that sometimes happened as he listened to Mrs. Worthington talk about her kindness to the pigeons. His old horse knew the way and he'd often dozed off along the road.

But never did he have so short a nap—and so strange a dream!

Why, it seemed they'd been going round and round— coach and all!

Mr. Bill climbed down from his seat and helped Mrs. Worthington out of the coach. She was busy picking up the cake crumbs that had scattered all over the inside of the coach.

"This road is getting bumpier than ever," she said. "It just goes to show how little attention anyone gives to the pigeons. I'm sure if more people traveled this way there'd be a lot of complaints—and these bumps and ruts in the road would have been fixed."

"Right you are, Mrs. Worthington," said Mr. Bill, picking up a crumb here and there.

After Mrs. Worthington had collected all her cake crumbs, even those in the corners of the coach cushions, she straightened her hat. Then, resting her hand lightly on Mr. Bill's arm, she stepped daintily to the frozen ground.

74

"Pidgy, pidgy, pidgy," she chirped as she threw handfuls of cake crumbs at the pigeons.

Only two sturdy young pigeons left their perch to fly down and strut about picking up crumbs. Most of the others had tucked their heads under their wings and gone back to sleep. A few, their eyes half-opened, sat up on their roosts frowning down at Arab, Mr. Bill, and particularly Mrs. Worthington.

"They haven't much appetite tonight," said Mr. Bill.

"And these are such good cake crumbs," said Mrs. Worthington wistfully. "Nut cake."

"Maybe it's this ice on the ground," said Mr. Bill. "Maybe they'd rather go hungry than get their feet cold."

They stood there awhile as Mrs. Worthington coaxed the pigeons and sadly scattered the last of the cake crumbs. It had

become much colder and a sharp wind blew most of the crumbs away. The two brave pigeons who had come down to peck away at Mrs. Worthington's nut-cake crumbs flew up to the roost and elbowed their way back into the tight line of pigeons already asleep there.

"I believe you're right, Mr. William," said Mrs. Worthington as Mr. Bill helped her back into the coach. "You must be right. And why should the little darlings chill their little pink feet? Do you know what I'm going to do?"

"No?" said Mr. Bill, shivering as he waited and anxious to be off.

The wind was really bad now and the rain had turned to sleet.

"I'm going to make each one of them a pair of woolen bed slippers," said Mrs. Worthington, with a gay little laugh. "Then they can hop down and have their crumbs and warm feet too. I'll begin knitting right now."

"Good idea," said Mr. Bill, and mumbling "Br-r-r, what a night," he started to climb up to his coach seat.

"Do you think red would be a good color?" she asked.

"Which?" asked Mr. Bill.

"For the pigeons' bed slippers, I mean. Would they like red?"

"Oh yes, indeed. Red's a fine color." And Mr. Bill quickly scrambled up to his seat.

Mr. Bill pulled his head as far down as he could into the collar of his greatcoat as a protection from the cold wind and cutting sleet.

Then, gathering up his reins, he said, "Giddap, Old Horse. Let's get out of this park quick." He bent his head against the wind and slapped the reins.

Arab wasted no time. He raced off into the face of that terrific wind. And in a few minutes he stood in front of the big hotel where Mrs. Worthington lived.

Of course he had whirled and swirled in his usual manner and gone up and down and round and round. But Mr. Bill, who had kept his head buried into the collar of his greatcoat, with his eyes shut tight, felt the cold wind and sleet more than he did Arab's dizzy whirling. The trip back couldn't be quick enough to suit him. Once when the back wheels of the coach had just scraped the top of some dogwood trees he had opened one eye and shut it again quickly. And Mrs. Worthington, bouncing around inside the coach, had noticed nothing. She was too busy with her knitting.

Mr. Bill helped her down to the sidewalk.

"Oh! Do look, Mr. William," she said proudly. And she opened her tiny fist to show him a knotted little lump of red wool.

"What is it?" asked Mr. Bill.

"The first pigeon bed slipper. Finished! Isn't it beautiful?"

"Very pretty," said Mr. Bill. "You're a quick knitter."

77

"Oh, thank you, Mr. William. Now good night, Mr. William," she said. "Tomorrow we ride again. I shall have all the slippers done." And off she tripped into her hotel.

" 'Night, Mrs. Worthington," Mr. Bill called after her. "Our best customer," he told Arab. "Now let's have one more pipe with the men, Old Horse. Then we'll be off to bed."

And he led Arab across the street again to the coachmen's fire.

9. Three Men from the Circus

THERE WAS A STRANGE COMMOTION going on around the coachmen's fire when Mr. Bill and Arab crossed over to the curb on the park side of the street.

And, though there was only one coach along the curb, there was quite a group gathered around the fire. The book-reading coachman, with the fingers of one hand stuck in his book, to keep his place, and a frankfurter sandwich in his other hand, was the center of it.

"No, gentlemen. No, sir!" he was saying as Mr. Bill joined the group. "I won't listen to no such proposition as that. I've gotta wait right here for a very important customer. Please go away."

Mr. Bill, without a word, moved up close to the fire barrel and spread his cold hands over the flame.

The three men turned to look at Mr. Bill. There were only three of them, though they had waved their hands so much, as they talked, it seemed like more.

"Are you a coachman?" asked the tallest one.

Mr. Bill warmed his hands a moment as he gazed into the fire. Then he looked up.

"What do I look like?" he asked.

"Have you got a horse—an intelligent horse?"

"Ach," said Mr. Bill scornfully. "Sure I have a fine intelligent horse. And a fine coach too." And he pointed back to Arab at the curb.

They all jerked their heads around and stared at Arab. Never since he left Arabia had he seen such bright-checked coats and such varicolored hats as they wore.

"Right," said the tall man, and he waved his hands and arms at his companions. Then he shouted, "Let me handle this. Let me handle it."

"I'll come to the point right away, Mr. Coachman," he said to Mr. Bill. "I'll tell you what we're gonna do."

"The name's Mr. Bill," said Mr. Bill.

"Mr. Chill?"

"No! Mr. Bill."

"Right," said the tall man. "I'm Mr. Right. This is Mr.

Axe . . . and here's Mr. Zee. Mr. Bill, meet Mr. Axe. Mr. Bill, meet Mr. Zee. Mr. Axe and Mr. Zee, meet Mr. Bill."

They all shook hands and mumbled, "Pleased to meet you."

"Right you are," said the tall Mr. Right. "Let's come right to the point, Mr. Bill. Can't waste a minute. Right? Time is fleeting. Every minute counts."

Then, after many more "rights" and quite a few quotations on how important it was not to waste time, Mr. Right explained they were all circus men from the World's Greatest Three-Ringed Circus Company. He added, "The greatest indoor show on earth." Tonight—that very night they were giving their first performance at the big Indoor Garden.

"And to come to the point at once, Mr. Bill," said Mr. Right. "We want to hire your horse for just half an hour."

"Not the coach?" asked Mr. Bill.

"Right! Just the horse, Mr. Bill."

"Just the horse, hey?" said Mr. Bill. Then he looked up at Mr. Right suspiciously. "You don't happen to know Mr. Gorman, do you?"

"Mr. Gorman?" said the surprised Mr. Right. "Never had the pleasure of meeting the gentleman."

"That's strange," said Mr. Bill. "He hires horses only for half-hours, too."

"Let's get back to business, Mr. Bill. We want to hire your horse. That's all. And we're prepared to pay well."

"What do you want to hire him for? Practice?" asked Mr. Bill.

"Practice? Why, no," said Mr. Right. "We hope he doesn't need any practice. We haven't time for that. Time is of the essence. Every minute's precious. Right?"

Then after many more "rights" and more talk about the importance of time, the tall circus man, Mr. Right, explained why they had to hire Mr. Bill's horse—right now. In fact, this very minute.

One of the performing horses had slipped and sprained one of his hind legs. He was one of those horses who go round and round in the center rings of the circus while the acrobats stand on his back and do their fancy tricks.

"Before we waste another minute," said Mr. Right, "we must make sure of one thing. Is your horse well trained? Can he go round and round—always turning right—and not get dizzy?"

Mr. Bill looked over at Arab. Then he turned back to Mr. Right.

"Mr. Right," he said slowly, "after what's been happening tonight, I'm beginning to think that's one of the things he can do best."

"Right," said Mr. Right. Then he looked at his big wrist watch. "Can't wait another minute. That act begins at ten-fifteen sharp. Here's the proposition, Mr. Bill—we stand ready to offer you five dollars to hire your horse for a half-hour. Take it or leave it. Right now."

Five dollars for his horse without the coach! Mr. Bill had never earned more than two dollars for his horse, coach, himself, and his whip.

Since he was a good businessman he said, "You've hired yourself a horse, mister."

And after Mr. Bill made the circus men promise not to take off the plaid blanket coat and hat Arab wore—so he'd not catch cold—the big business deal was closed.

Now what of Arab while this argument was going on? What do you think? Naturally he was delighted.

"Well, now," he thought. "Now I'll really see the city. We can't ride through the dark park to get to that circus. At last I'll see the city—and the circus too!"

He trembled with glee. And he was ready to dash off with his big round-and-round loops the moment they unhitched him from the shafts.

"And I'll show Mr. Right I can go round and round, all right," thought Arab.

83

But the circus men had other ideas. They backed up a big truck. Quickly they lifted Arab into it (they were surprised how light he was) and they drove off at a good clip to the circus. Down the big avenue, across the crowded broad street —and they pulled up to the back entrance of an immense building.

It was bigger than any building Arab had seen along the way. He had looked out of the truck window as they sped along. And he saw all the wonderful things Old Coach Horse had told him about all through the summer. The tall buildings, the beautiful shopwindows, the brightly lit better-class restaurants—and even what must have been the big library. Yes, it must have been the big library; for he saw the stone lions—the coach horse had mentioned them—crouched along the broad steps. They looked so intellectual!

"What an experience!" said Arab to himself. "And now the circus."

10. The Most Wonderful Trick

THE TRUCK WAS DRIVEN right into the wide doors. They lifted Arab down to the sawdust-covered ground inside the big building. Then they quickly fastened a small wooden platform on his back, and he was ready.

The children who used to stand along the line waiting for their turn on the merry-go-round had talked about the circus. At that time Arab had been just a little doubtful. Nothing could possibly be as beautiful, as colorful, as exciting, as the children said everything was at the circus.

As he stood in that room looking around at the busy sight,

Arab decided the children were unfair to circuses. The circus was even more wonderful than they said.

This room was the one through which all the circus people and animals passed on their way to the big arena. It was full of animals and people dressed up in many-colored costumes—all going in different directions.

"Why, there . . ." said Arab to himself. "There are the jugglers . . . the acrobats . . . the Indians . . . the brave lion tamers . . . and everybody the children talked about. And here come the clowns—the best of all!"

Out of the big lighted arena came a lot of people dressed
in immense hats, flopping shoes, strange wide-striped trousers
—and all their faces were so funny with their red noses and
painted mouths that Arab laughed out loud.

A man at the door shouted, "O.K. Horse acrobats. You're
on."

Some people dressed in pink tights ran out into the arena.
Then followed some big white horses with platforms tied to
their backs just like the one Arab had on his. A man grabbed
Arab's bridle and led him out into the brilliant glare. He had
a little difficulty getting Arab to go in the right direction. But

after three or four other men came to help, the man leading Arab got him into the ring where he was to perform.

The ringmaster, standing there, murmured to the man, "Hey, what's going on here? Don't you fellows know the clown act's over?"

The man holding Arab's bridle said, "The regular horse sprained his leg. You'll have to put on your act with this one."

The ringmaster looked Arab over. Then he shook his head.

"What a horse!" he said.

Arab didn't mind. He was happily looking at all the exciting things around him. A big band started playing a lively march.

The ringmaster snapped his whip in the air and said to Arab, "Get going, Horse. Let's see if you can go round."

"Can I go round? Ha!" laughed Arab to himself, and round and round he went—twice as fast as any of the horses in any of the other rings.

"Whoa. Take it easy," said the ringmaster. "You'll do."

And Arab went round and round at half speed.

One of the acrobats, dressed in pink tights, hopped into Arab's ring and made a deep bow to the people sitting on the benches, first on one side and then the other. Then he turned to the ringmaster.

"Where's my regular horse?" he whispered "What's this old clown doing in my ring?"

"Your regular hurt his leg," answered the ringmaster. "You've got a good horse here. He has real talent. Give him a chance."

Arab was proud that the ringmaster could see he had talent for circus work. He wondered how one goes about getting a steady job in the circus.

The music changed to a fast waltz.

The ringmaster snapped his whip again and said "Ready now" to the acrobat. And the act began.

The acrobat jumped nimbly onto the platform that was strapped to Arab's back. He balanced himself for a moment there. Then he turned a somersault in the air and landed on Arab's back again.

"He'll do," said the acrobat. "But the old clown's slow. Whip him up a bit."

The ringmaster snapped his whip a few times at Arab's slow-trotting hoofs.

"Very well, gentlemen," chuckled Arab, "here we go!"

And round and round he went. Up and down, and round and round! And so fast did he go that while the acrobat was still in the air, turning one somersault, Arab had circled the ring at least three times. And he was careful too. He always caught the acrobat on his back as he'd complete a somersault. His up-and-down movement as he raced around helped too. It threw the acrobat even higher into the air so that Arab sometimes sped five times around that ring before the acrobat came down on his back!

It was the most wonderful trick anyone had ever seen in the circus!

The audience applauded and cheered. They all neglected the main act in the center ring to crane their necks and watch the wonderful Arab and his acrobat. The star performer, the acrobat in the center ring, who had been jumping with great skill from one racing horse to another as they sped around his ring—even he soon stopped doing tricks to watch them too.

Everyone was watching and admiring Arab and his acrobat now. Even some men who had been flying overhead from one swinging trapeze to another just sat on their trapeze and clapped their hands.

The band played faster and faster!

The big spotlight was switched on so that it lit up Arab's ring only!

Everything was going along marvelously, but it all ended very suddenly!

Arab was so happy to be racing around at top speed and tossing his acrobat higher and higher into the air that he said to himself, "Now I'll show everyone something they'll remember forever! When my acrobat comes down again I'll toss him up so high that I'll race around this ring ten times before he comes down!"

And that's what he did!

At least he tossed his acrobat way up high—then sped around the ring ten times. And, since the acrobat hadn't come down yet, he tore around the ring ten times more. Round and round.

He could have kept it up all night if the band hadn't stopped playing so that he could hear the ringmaster's shouts: "Whoa, Horse. Whoa!"

Arab stood still.

Then he saw why his acrobat hadn't come down. He'd been tossed so high he'd gone right up to the trapeze swings near the ceiling. And the men sitting there had caught him, as he was passing by, before he crashed against the ceiling. He had been sitting there with them laughing and applauding while Arab raced around the ring by himself.

Then everybody laughed and cheered Arab. And a few men led him back to the entrance of the big arena.

"Some horse!" said the ringmaster. "He's got real talent."

11. The Lost Hallowe'en

Arab found Mr. Bill drowsily talking to the book-reading coachman when the circus truck had backed up to the corner near the park and unloaded him.

The circus men told Mr. Bill, "You've got a very talented horse here." Then they drove back to the Indoor Garden.

The strong wind had blown the clouds away. The rain and sleet had stopped. Now the night was clear and crisp.

Sleepy Mr. Bill hitched Arab onto the coach, shouted "Good night" to the book-reading coachman, and then led Arab back toward the old coach horse's stable.

The book-reading coachman returned to his book. He seemed just as happy that his important customer hadn't come around yet. He'd much rather read.

As he led Arab away Mr. Bill grumbled, "Now there, Old Horse, don't be so skittish. Stop that bounding about. . . . Drat this ice. We seem to keep turning."

Arab restrained himself and tried hard to keep from going up and down.

"Yes . . . you're a talented horse. Sure—you've a fine talent for pushing me around on this icy street."

Arab's mind was too full of his happy adventurous night to worry about Mr. Bill's grumbling. Anyway Mr. Bill didn't sound angry—just sleepy.

They went along the street, crossed over, and turned into the alley without too much trouble. Mr. Bill fell down only once. He led Arab up the alley and into Old Coach Horse's stable.

"We're home, Old Horse," said Mr. Bill.

Mr. Bill never turned the electric light on in the stable when he brought the coach in at night. There were cracks in the ceiling overhead and the stable light would shine through to his apartment upstairs. He always unharnessed the old coach horse in the dark as quietly as possible, so he'd not wake up his sleeping family.

That's what he did with Arab. And, after he had folded away the coach-horse blanket, he gave Arab a gentle pat in the darkness.

"Gawsh, you're getting harder and bonier than ever, Old Horse. Good night, Old Bag of Bones," he said affectionately.

Mr. Bill took his shoes off and silently climbed up the stairs.

Arab stood quietly in the darkness. He heard the gentle snores of the old coach horse snug in his bed of straw.

"Ah, what a night!" thought Arab. "Only in this great city could one have such adventure."

Arab went over all the things that had happened that night. He didn't linger long on Mr. Gorman's half-hour or Mrs. Worthington's ride; but at the circus, where everyone applauded and cheered his tricks—he went over every detail of that adventure, again and again.

What if he, Arab, were to get a steady job with the circus? Everyone said he had real talent. Why, this turning right, round and round, and going up and down which he had thought was just a habit—in the circus it was called talent. Maybe that's what it was—*talent!*

Why, it might be another gift—like his gift of speech and understanding which the coach horse had mentioned. Yes, what if he were to do tricks in the circus regularly? Get a steady job! Or maybe he'd go on the stage! And never return to the merry-go-round again. . . .

Arab dozed off and dreamed about the circus.

He was a healthy young wooden horse—he slept like a log.

The next morning the youngest Bill boy clattered down the stairs in a rush. He had to make up some schoolwork and he was up before the rest of the family. On this day he'd not

97

like to be kept after school to do his addition and subtraction examples over again. Not on this day—the day of the big parade!

He jumped the last three steps leading down to the stable and landed with an awful bang!

That woke Old Coach Horse up. He stumbled to his feet and stood blinking in the bright sunlight that streamed into the stable window. Arab was already up.

The youngest Bill stopped and stared with eyes as large as saucers at the two horses—the shaggy old coach horse covered with wisps of straw and Arab looking pretty shaggy too, with his paint peeled off in many places.

The two horses stared back at the youngest Bill.

"Hey! What's—where'd we get two horses? Hey, Pop!" shouted the youngest Bill.

Mr. Bill's head appeared at the head of the stairs.

"What's all the rumpus down there?"

"Come down, Pop," said the youngest Bill. "Look—two horses!"

Mr. Bill hurried down the stairs—followed by the whole Bill family.

They all looked at Arab in silence. The coach horse, after one pained glance at poor Arab, rolled his eyes away and blinked out the stable window.

"Well," said Mr. Bill, "where'd he come from? What kind of Hallowe'en joke is this?"

"Hallowe'en joke?" said the smallest Bill.

"Yes, Hallowe'en joke," said Mr. Bill angrily. "Yes, yes, I know last night was October thirtieth—Hallowe'en. I know! Now whose Hallowe'en joke was this? Bringing a scratched-up wooden horse into the stable!"

All the Bill children looked at one another in amazement. They had completely forgotten about Hallowe'en! Why, they all just studied their lessons and talked about Mr. Gorman's parade—and went to bed. Everybody had forgotten about Hallowe'en! It was either the cold rain or thinking about Mr. Gorman's parade. Now they'd have to wait a whole year before Hallowe'en came around again!

The youngest Bill's face crinkled up and he began to blubber.

"All right, so you didn't," said Mr. Bill. "Get along with you. Go on to school."

Now there was so much activity in the stable that neither Arab nor Coach Horse could do anything to mend their broken plans.

After much running up and down the stable stairs the rest of the Bill children got their hats, coats, breakfasts, and books —and raced off to school.

When the last of them had slammed out the door, Mr. Bill brought down the coach horse's porridge in a bucket. He'd eaten his with the children.

Again and again Arab had hissed over to Coach Horse staring out the stable window at a blank wall.

"What shall we do, Old One? What now?"

And the coach horse without turning his head always answered, "Shush, I'm thinking."

Just before he dipped his head into his bucket Old Horse said in a hollow voice:

> "Ah, the best-laid-plans of Horses and Men
> Are sometimes broken—now and then."

"Is that your own poem, Old One?" asked Arab.

"No, it's Shakespeare," said Coach Horse, and he quickly dipped his head into his breakfast—right up to his eyes.

Even the strange taste of the cod-liver oil mixed with his porridge didn't keep him from gulping it down. Anything was better than trying to answer Arab's insistent questions right now.

101

He kept his head dipped in his bucket long after he'd finished his breakfast—thinking and thinking. His was a slow mind and Arab's impatient "Now what will we do?" didn't help. And just when a vague idea was finally beginning to stir in Old Horse's head—the telephone rang!

Mr. Bill answered it with a businesslike "Yes . . . yes . . . yes. We'll be there." And he hung up the receiver.

"That was Mrs. Worthington, Old Horse," he said, picking up the coach horse's breakfast bucket. "She says the century plant's blooming in the Botanical Garden. She heard it on the radio. Hurry up and get harnessed—she doesn't want to miss it when it opens up."

And Mr. Bill went up to get his hat and coat.

"Can't I go in your place?" whispered Arab eagerly.

"Goodness no!" said Coach Horse, bustling around as he dressed himself. "Not after what happened this morning. You'd better stay right here."

"Alone?" asked Arab sadly.

"Don't be childish," said Coach Horse impatiently. "I can't afford to lose this job. You'd better stay here and trot back to your merry-go-round when it gets dark again. Sh-h-h. Here comes Mr. Bill."

Mr. Bill came down the stairs quickly. Arab still stood between the shafts where Mr. Bill had unharnessed him in the dark.

"You're still here, hey?" said Mr. Bill to Arab. "Well, move out of those shafts." And he grabbed Arab around the neck, took a deep breath, and pulled hard.

Over went Arab! Over went Mr. Bill, and he sat down on the stable floor—hard! He'd used too much strength on the light Arab.

How was he to know that wonder wood, though it's lively and hard as iron, is the lightest wood in the world—lighter than cork? Mr. Bill had never been to Arabia.

He picked himself up and stood for a moment looking down at Arab lying stiff on the stable floor. Slowly he bent

over and hefted Arab's weight gently once or twice. Then he stooped and picked Arab up, carried him into Coach Horse's stall, and dropped him on the pile of straw.

"Must be hollow," he mumbled. "There's no doubt about it. Any boy could have carried him in to play this Halloween joke."

Quickly Mr. Bill backed the coach horse into the shafts, snapped on his harness—and off they went. Coach Horse was glad to get away from Arab's accusing, sad eyes.

Arab spent a dull listless morning in the stable. There was nothing to see out of the windows. Anyway they faced the blank brick walls of the alley. He nudged the door open and looked down toward the street. And that's where Mr. Bill found him when he returned for his lunch!

"What goes on here?" said Mr. Bill angrily. "Who moved you out of that stall?"

He shouted up to Mrs. Bill. Had she moved the wooden horse about? She called down from the head of the stairs that she'd been busy ironing all morning—hadn't had time to clean up the stable yet.

"Well, never mind. It must be that Hallowe'en jokemaker again," said Mr. Bill. "Fix up Old Horse's salad—and a small plate for Mrs. Worthington. She's sitting out in the coach. No radishes in her salad, please—only lettuce."

Then he turned and glared at Arab.

"And now I'll fix you," he said. "Hallowe'en jokes! Ach!"

He picked Arab up and carried him down the alley to the street, and he tossed him—none too gently—among a number of trash barrels. Then he stumped up the alley again.

12. The Toyshop Parade

ARAB WAS NOT VERY COMFORTABLE. Slowly he wiggled around so that he could rest easier against the barrels and could see what went on around him. At least this was better than being shut up in the stable, he thought.

The janitor from one of the brick buildings that made up one side of the alley climbed out of his cellar and dumped an old mattress down on Arab and the barrels. The janitor hadn't even given Arab a look—to him trash was trash.

"Better and better," said Arab to himself. He pushed the old mattress away from his head so he could see the street again.

106

It was a brisk sunny day. There were quite a few people lined up on both sides of the street at the curb. People either too young or too old to be in school. Arab wondered why they were there. Then he remembered.

"The parade. That's what they're waiting for," he said. "Why, I'll be able to see the parade too! Not the marchers maybe, but surely the big balloons."

And that's why Mrs. Worthington was there too.

The coach with Mrs. Worthington in it was drawn up to the curb at the entrance to the alley. The top of the coach was down and Arab could see Mrs. Worthington happily knitting away at her pigeons' bed slippers. Her lap held quite a pile of little red woolen lumps—like the sample pigeon slipper she had shown Mr. Bill last night.

"It's all right knitting them," thought Arab. "But who's going to get them on the pigeons' feet, Mr. Bill?" And he laughed to himself as he pictured Mr. Bill chasing pigeons to fit them into their slippers.

His old friend Coach Horse sagged so between his shafts that they seemed to be holding him up. His old brow was puckered in thought.

"The Old One must be worried about me," said Arab to himself, and he stopped himself just in time from calling to the coach horse.

Just then Mr. Bill came down the alley carrying a big nose-bag full of salad for Coach Horse and a tiny plate of lettuce leaves for Mrs. Worthington.

107

"It's lovely, Mr. William," she cried. "And so much of it. I shan't be able to finish."

"Try your best," said Mr. Bill, and he climbed up on his coach seat to smoke his pipe.

He'd already had his lunch.

"Why, there's Mr. Gorman," chirped Mrs. Worthington between two bites of lettuce.

"Mr. Gorman! No?" said Mr. Bill. "Can't be. He's going to lead this parade."

"But he is there," said Mrs. Worthington. "There between those two big baby carriages at the curb."

Mr. Bill stood up.

"Sure, I see him too. Hey! Mr. Gorman!" he shouted.

Mr. Gorman pretended he didn't hear a thing. But when Mr. Bill had bellowed his name a few more times Mr. Gorman slid out of his hiding place and limped over to the coach. He had a pink cushion under his arm. "Compliments of the Gorman Toyshop" was embroidered on one side of it.

"Come, sit here beside me," said Mrs. Worthington. "We ought to have a wonderful view of the parade."

Mr. Gorman nodded, climbed into the coach, laid his cushion on the seat, and sat down on it slowly.

"Now we're all comfortable," said Mrs. Worthington.

Mr. Gorman sat there with a faraway look in his pale blue eyes. He didn't say a word—just nodded or shook his head as the occasion demanded. Mrs. Worthington clicked away with her needles and chatted about her pigeons.

Once she said something that she thought deserved more

108

than a yes or no answer—something about public bird baths for pigeons. But Mr. Gorman neither nodded nor shook his head. He just looked off into the distance.

"Has the pussycat got your tongue, Mr. Gorman?" she asked, with a sweet smile.

Mr. Gorman turned and thrust out his underlip at Mrs. Worthington.

"It's my lip," he said. "Can't talk—it hurts."

"Why, it's cut," said Mrs. Worthington sympathetically.

"Must have bit it," said Mr. Gorman. "Last night—practicing." Then he shut up again.

More and more people gathered along the curb. School was out early and the boys and girls were mixed in the crowd. Everybody waited impatiently now for the parade to begin.

Mr. Bill took his pipe out of his mouth and said, "It's a fine day for balloons, Mr. Gorman."

"Too windy," said Mr. Gorman.

"We'll have a fine sight of the floats from here," said Mr. Bill.

"Maybe," said Mr. Gorman.

Mr. Bill was silent for a moment. Then he squinted one eye and faced Mr. Gorman.

"Mr. Gorman, is there or isn't there going to be a parade?"

Mr. Gorman nodded.

"Well, now. I don't want to offend. But how is it you're sitting with us? Not that you're not welcome. Thought you were going to lead."

"I'm not going to lead the parade," said Mr. Gorman as he sadly shrugged his shoulders. "There's no fun leading a parade in an automobile. Don't think the boys and girls would have liked it either. They like horses. Well, since I didn't practice enough, I can't ride—so I'm not leading."

Mr. Gorman had forgotten his hurt underlip as he talked. His heart was heavy.

They sat there waiting in silence for the parade to begin.

"Here it comes!" shouted some boys.

Then everyone heard the bands. Soon the parade swung along past the coach.

Arab couldn't see who was leading the parade from where he lay under the mattress. In fact, he could not see much of the parade at all. Only the big balloons that were being pulled along the street by clowns.

But they were very beautiful!

Mr. Gorman's lip seemed to have become all better now. He was telling Mrs. Worthington and Mr. Bill about the new Forty-story Toyshop. His eyes lit up with excitement as he described the wonderful things in his fine new building.

Arab missed a lot of what he was saying, because of the bands and the laughter of the children along the curb; but he heard clearly Mr. Gorman's description of the modern playground that was built up on the roof. There were sliding ponds, sand piles, wading pools, seesaws, swings, flowers, and even fruit trees up there. The flowers and trees would bloom even in the wintertime.

"Really!" said Mrs. Worthington.

"Yes," said Mr. Gorman. "You see, it's all enclosed in nonbreakable glass. And it's heated so that children can play without wearing heavy coats and mufflers."

"Well, I never," said Mrs. Worthington. "And have you any birds up there? Pigeons?"

"We'll put some in," said Mr. Gorman.

Then he went on to explain how the top of the glass-enclosed playground rolled back on sunny days—and all the other modern features.

"Yes, it's all very up-to-date," said Mr. Gorman. "But it's not perfect yet. There's something missing."

"Sounds O.K. to me," said Mr. Bill.

"Indeed it does," said Mrs. Worthington.

"No, it's not perfect," said Mr. Gorman. "I'm not sure children like everything new and shiny, the way it is up on that roof. We ought to have something—maybe just one thing—a little more old-fashioned."

Mr. Gorman was looking at Mrs. Worthington's hat when he said that. It didn't bother her. She agreed heartily with him. So did Mr. Bill.

"That's true," said Mrs. Worthington. "Something old. Something new. Something borrowed. Something blue."

Mr. Gorman couldn't understand what Mrs. Worthington's poem had to do with what he was talking about. He continued.

"I mean—say if we had a weather vane up there. Just a good old-fashioned weather vane, like we used to have on my father's barn when I was a boy. A horse weather vane. . . . It would have to be a pretty good size of course, but—"

"Did you say a horse weather vane?" asked Mr. Bill.

"Yes."

"Come with me," said Mr. Bill mysteriously, and down he climbed from his seat. "Come along. I think I know just the thing."

Mr. Gorman followed Mr. Bill through the crowd on the sidewalk to the pile of trash up against the brick wall.

"Now. Where is he?" said Mr. Bill. "That horse never stays put. Ah, here he is." And Mr. Bill lifted the mattress to display the surprised Arab to Mr. Gorman.

113

"Course he's a bit battered—not in the best condition. But he is a horse," said Mr. Bill.

Mr. Gorman studied Arab carefully.

"Just the thing!" he cried. "Fine. Fine. And he's really in good condition. There's nothing the matter with him a coat of paint won't fix."

"Yes, sir," said Mr. Bill.

"What's he made of?" asked Mr. Gorman, and before Mr. Bill could answer he reached over and tapped Arab's head with his knuckles. Clunk!

"Why, he's made of iron!" said Mr. Gorman.

"Wrong," said Mr. Bill. "He's wood—and hollow too, I think. He's as light as a feather. Look here."

Mr. Bill pushed the trash aside and with almost no effort picked Arab up in his arms.

"See," he said. "He's as light as a feather. Hold him yourself." And he thrust Arab into astonished Mr. Gorman's arms.

"So he is," said Mr. Gorman. "I can carry him easily, and I'm not a strong man."

"Yes, sir," said Mr. Bill.

"Tell you what," said Mr. Gorman. "Let's take him over to the Forty-story Toyshop—at once. We can get someone to paint him up with a coat of gold paint. And we can set him up in the playground before the parade ends."

"Good idea," said Mr. Bill. "I'll give you a hand carrying him."

"No, no," said Mr. Gorman. "I can manage him easily. Come along."

And off they marched along the sidewalk toward the Forty-story Toyshop.

Mrs. Worthington hopped out of the coach and followed them too. She wanted to see if there was room for a pigeon roost up on the playground.

They made quite a parade of their own as they walked along—Mr. Gorman leading, and not riding his horse as he'd planned. On the contrary, it looked as if his horse was riding Mr. Gorman!

115

He carried Arab high over his head so that Arab's hoofs would not hurt anyone in the crowd. Close at his heels was Mr. Bill, carrying his long whip with its pink bow on top. Then Mrs. Worthington, knitting as she walked. Some little boys followed along, and more and more of them tagged on until there was as big a parade marching along the sidewalk as there was in the middle of the street.

13. Arab is a Hero

So Mr. Gorman led his parade right up to the door of his big new toyshop.

Arab's old paint was sandpapered away and he was quickly brushed with a fine gold paint. Then some of Mr. Gorman's workmen set him up on a high pole in the center of a flower bed in Mr. Gorman's wonderful playground on top of the Forty-story Toyshop.

"There," said Mr. Gorman when the last nail had been driven and the last screw tightened. "There's as handsome an old-fashioned weather vane as ever I saw."

It all happened so quickly Arab didn't know what to think. And, if he had thought about it, I don't imagine it would have mattered. Mr. Gorman was a very determined little man.

Fortunately Arab liked his new job. He had enjoyed being carried over the bobbing heads of the crowd. Not only the ride—but he really did get a good look at the parade.

And, now that he was up on this tall pole on top of the Forty-story Toyshop, Arab was delighted. He could see not only the whole city but far beyond. The park was spread out below him like an immense carpet. The broad roads were now laid out like silver ribbons. There were evergreens, white birches, and leafless brown trees and bushes spotted here and there on the lawns. The park lake glittered in the sun—a beautiful blue jewel.

He could see Mr. Timothy's merry-go-round tucked away in its clump of trees. How tiny it looked! How precious and small everything looked!

Arab whirled with delight round and round on his tall pole.

"What a job this is! I'm a weather vane!" he said to himself. "How wonderful to be up here!" And he slowed down a bit as he thought. "I wonder what a weather vane is supposed to do?"

Mr. Gorman and his mechanics were tinkering with some machinery at the base of Arab's tall pole. Mrs. Worthington and Mr. Bill, who had come along up on the elevator, stood around giving advice.

"Maybe you ought to put a little sand in those bearings," said Mr. Bill. "That's no way for a weather vane to act. Whirling around like that."

"Indeed," said Mrs. Worthington. "How is anyone ever to know how the wind blows? See those flags. The wind's definitely from the north. And that horse points toward the East River! Really!"

Mr. Gorman lifted his flushed face and squinted up at Arab.

"Yes, but you know . . ." he said slowly. "The weather vane on my father's barn used to act like that sometimes."

"Oh, so that's what I'm doing up here!" said Arab to himself. "A weather vane must show how the wind blows. Very well."

And he let the wind blow him around until Mrs. Worthington and Mr. Bill were satisfied he acted like a real weather vane.

"There now," said Mr. Bill. "He's working perfect. Guess the sand in those bearings helped."

But Arab was not the perfect weather vane very long. Out of the corner of his eye he had noticed something very strange in the clump of trees that surrounded the old merry-go-round. Why, it seemed they were bursting into bloom with a lot of tiny brilliant yellow and red flowers!

Why, that was impossible! Specially at this time of the year. Arab stopped being a good weather vane long enough to whirl around and take a good look.

119

Yes! It did look as if red and yellow flowers were quickly blooming on the topmost branches of those trees. More and more of them appeared.

Suddenly Arab realized they were not flowers! They were bursts of flame!

Why, those trees were afire!

The old merry-go-round was in danger!

What could he do? How could he tell those people standing there worrying about wind directions? None of them could understand Horse Arabic.

He whirled round and round in distress. Oh, poor Mr. Timothy! Oh, the poor children—and the horses!

He stopped whirling and turned toward the merry-go-round. The topmost branches of the trees were all aflame now. Down at the foot of his pole there was a great to-do.

"Seems like you didn't get enough sand in those bearings yet," said Mr. Bill. "Your weather vane's off once more. He's pointing against the wind again."

"It seems to me," sniffed Mrs. Worthington, "with much

less trouble they could have put a pigeon roost up on that pole instead of a horse weather vane. Particularly one that just whirls round and round instead of pointing to the East River as it should. Look now—he's pointing out toward the park." And Mrs. Worthington looked out over the park as she talked. "Fire! It's a fire!" she screamed.

Mr. Gorman, deep in the machinery at the base of the pole, said, "Can't be. Not in this modern building. It's fireproof, waterproof, soundproof, got unbreakable glass, three hundred and seventy-one telephones, escalators with seats—"

"Not here!" screamed Mrs. Worthington. "It's out in the park—the pigeon roosts! I feel faint."

Mr. Bill looked out in the direction Arab pointed.

"It's the old merry-go-round," he bellowed.

Mr. Gorman jumped to his feet and took just one look. Then he dashed off to one of his three hundred and seventy-one telephones. He called the fire department and raced out to the park wearing his fire hat. He was a deputy assistant fireman and always drove to fires with the Mayor.

Arab on his pole breathed a deep sigh of relief. Already he could see the fire engines speeding like shiny beetles along the ribbonlike park roads. A very short time after, the firemen were fighting the blaze . . . and the fire was out. Just a few wisps of smoke drifted up from the trees.

The merry-go-round had been saved!

"Mr. Gorman might not be a good rider," said Arab. "But he does make a fine fireman."

There were a lot of happy voices down on the roof now. Mr. Gorman had returned and brought with him Mr. Timothy, the merry-go-round man, and a lot of children.

It seems they all had run as fast as they could into the park when they heard good Mr. Timothy's horses were in danger. But none of them except Mr. Timothy got there in time. On the way back Mr. Gorman had met the children as they puffed along the road to the merry-go-round and he piled them into his automobile and into the fire trucks. And here they were.

Right then and there Mr. Gorman gave a party to celebrate everything at once. The opening of his toyshop, the parade, the merry-go-round's being saved, and last but not least—Arab!

Everybody had cocoa in paper cups and cake on paper plates. Mrs. Worthington helped serve. She went around telling everyone who would listen that if it hadn't been for Arab the merry-go-round would have burned up. And she didn't forget her pigeons in the excitement, for she collected quite a few cake crumbs.

At last the party was over and everyone went home.

Arab was alone on his high pole atop the tallest toyshop in the world.

The sun set, the sky darkened, and the stars began to twinkle all around him. Overhead, heaven-made stars. Down below him, in the buildings and along the streets, those made by men.

"At last," said Arab, "I have found my place in the world. I shall never travel again."

And he never did!

But on some moonlit winter nights, while the old coach horse stood along the curb at the corner of the park, he'd hear

an old Arabian song carried on the wind. And he'd chuckle to himself, for he knew Arab was whirling around on his pole singing "The Song of the Lonely Stallion."

> Out into the moonlit night I run.
> I drink from the Moon Pools—alone, alone.

And do you know, aside from you and me and Old Coach Horse, there are only two other people who know that the gold-painted horse who whirls around atop Mr. Gorman's Forty-story Toyshop is Arab? Those two other people are a little girl who was at the party and recognized Arab through his gold paint—and Mr. Timothy. She had whispered it to him. And good Mr. Timothy had patted her head. Then he looked up at Arab and just smiled as he said, "Maybe when spring comes he'll come back."